D0576917

2016

University Branch

NO LONGER PROPERTY OF
SEATTLE PUBLIC LIBRARY

If an

ARMADILLO

Went to a

RESTAURANT

ELLEN FISCHER

If an ARMADILLO Went to a RESTAURANT

Illustrations by
LAURA WOOD

SCARLETTA KIDS

MINNEAPOLIS, MINNESOTA

Text copyright ©2014 Ellen Fischer

Illustrations copyright ©2014 Laura Wood

Published by Scarletta Kids, an imprint of Scarletta

This book is a work of fiction. Names, characters, places, events, and incidents are either a product of the author's imagination or are used fictitiously. Any resemblance to reality is entirely coincidental.

All rights reserved. No part of this book may be used or reproduced in any manner whatsoever without written permission except in the case of brief quotations embodied in critical articles and reviews. For information, write to Scarletta, 10 South Fifth Street, Suite 1105, Minneapolis, MN 55402, U.S.A, www.scarlettapress.com.

Guided Reading Level: Guided Reading Level – M (Developmental Reading Assessment 30)

Library of Congress Cataloging-in-Publication Data

Fischer, Ellen, 1947–

If an armadillo went to a restaurant
by Ellen Fischer : illustrated by Laura Wood.

     pages cm

Summary: Illustrations and easy-to-read text explore what various animals, from an armadillo in an underground restaurant to a wallaby in a sandwich shop, might choose to eat.

ISBN 978-1-938063-39-8 (hardcover) --
ISBN 978-1-938063-40-4 (ebook) --
ISBN 978-1-938063-41-1 (nook book)

1. Animals--Food--Fiction. 2. Food habits--Fiction. 3. Restaurants--Fiction. 4. Humorous stories. I. Wood, Laura, 1985- illustrator. II. Title.

PZ7.F498766If 2014

    E   --dc23

                              2013037111

Book design by Anders Hanson, Mighty Media, Inc.

Printed and manufactured in the United States
North Mankato, MN
Distributed by Publishers Group West

First edition

10 9 8 7 6 5 4 3 2 1

ELLEN FISCHER grew up in St. Louis, Missouri, but has lived in North Carolina for over thirty years. She loves to teach and write for children. She has taught elementary age children for over twenty years and is the mother of three.

LAURA WOOD is a illustrator living in Melbourne, Australia. She has a passion for catlike animals, flat shoes, and good food. When she is not busy making pictures, she drinks tea, watches movies, and spends time with the people she loves.

Dedicated with Love
to **EZRA** and **WILL.**

- E.L.F.

If an ARMADILLO burrowed into an underground restaurant, what would she order?

An armadillo might order ...

A plate of

ANTS AND WORMS

with a few beetles thrown in.

If a **SEA TURTLE** crawled into a lagoon buffet, what would he order?

Fried chicken with gravy?

NO SIR!

A sea turtle might order ...

Crabs and shrimp

WITH A JELLYFISH ON TOP

If a **RATTLESNAKE** slithered through a desert cafeteria, what would she choose?

Beans and rice? ACTUALLY, NO.

A rattlesnake
might choose ...

Several rodents
and a lizard.

WHOLE WOULD BE BEST!

If a **BUTTERFLY** fluttered to a garden cafe, what would he order?

A bowl of oatmeal?

SURELY NOT.

A butterfly might order...

A BOWL OF LILAC NECTAR ... hold the flower.

If a WALLABY hopped to an Australian sandwich shop, what would she order?

A hamburger with french fries?

DEFINITELY NOT!

GRASSES AND LEAVES

A wallaby might order...

... for two.

If a **HEDGEHOG** stopped by a forest food court, what would she select?

Lasagna with
a side salad?

IMPROBABLE.

A hedgehog
might select ...

A plate of
crunchy
beetles
with
three
sides ...

If an OSTRICH ran to a grassland grill, what would she order?

A BLT on whole wheat?

HIGHLY DEBATABLE.

An ostrich might order ...

A mix of

SUCCULENT PLANTS AND STONE ... TO GO

... no water necessary.

If a GIRAFFE stuck his neck into a savanna snack bar, what would he order?

Pepperoni pizza?

NOPE.

A giraffe   might order ...

ONE LARGE APRICOT TREE

with a bucket of water to wash it down.

If an **OCTOPUS** swam to an ocean eatery, what would she request?

A bowl of chili? **TOO HOT!**

An octopus might request ...

A bowl of scallops, snails, and crabs.
EIGHT FORKS, PLEASE.

If I went to MY favorite restaurant, what would I order?

A plate of ants and worms?

I would order ...

A stack of
BLUEBERRY PANCAKES
with a tall glass of milk.

What would YOU order?

✗ BREAKFAST ✗

Ham and Cheese OMELET
Chocolate Chip PANCAKES
Fresh Berries with YOGURT

✗ LUNCH ✗

MACARONI and Cheese
PB&J SANDWICH
Fresh SALAD
Chicken Noodle SOUP

✗ DINNER ✗

Veggie LASAGNA
Bacon CHEESEBURGER
Chicken TACOS
Grilled Cheese SANDWICH
Pineapple PIZZA
SPAGHETTI & Meatballs

✗ DESSERT ✗

ICE CREAM Sundae
Chocolate CAKE